By Margaret Wise Brown

Pictures by Garth Williams

Originally published as *The Golden Sleepy Book*

A GOLDEN BOOK, NEW YORK
Western Publishing Company, Inc., Racine, Wisconsin 53404

Acknowledgment

The author learned the song *All the Pretty Little Horses* in this book from Mammy Ludy Ludy Hinton and Sugar Meat Hinton of Halifax, Virginia. A somewhat different version has been copyrighted by the late John Lomax. The version in this book is printed with his kind permission.

MARGARET WISE BROWN is one of the best-known and most prolific authors of books for children. Her sensitive, lively, tender, and often amusing stories have delighted both youngsters and their parents for generations. At one point in her career, Margaret Wise Brown decided to stop writing, but fortunately she found that she could not stop and eventually published more than eighty-five books. Among them are many well-loved Golden Books, including such enduring favorites as *Home for a Bunny, The Sailor Dog,* and *The Friendly Book.*

Born in New York, GARTH WILLIAMS had an extensive art education and early career interests in architecture, theatrical scenery design, oil painting, poster design, and sculpture. In 1945, he illustrated his first children's book, *Stuart Little.* Since then, his imaginative, endearing art work has enhanced more than fifty children's books. In addition to the Margaret Wise Brown books listed above, Garth Williams illustrated *Three Bedtime Stories, My Big Golden Counting Book, The Tiny Golden Library,* and many other popular Golden Books.

J

THE WHISPERING RABBIT

ONCE there was a sleepy little rabbit
Who began to yawn—
And he yawned and he yawned and he yawned and he yawned,
"Hmmm ————————"

He opened his little rabbit mouth when he yawned till you could see his white front teeth and his little round pink mouth, and he yawned and he yawned until suddenly a bee flew into his mouth and he swallowed the bee.

"Hooo — hooo —," said a fat old owl. "Always keep your paw in front of your mouth when you yawn," hooted the owl.

"Rabbits never do that," said the sleepy little rabbit.

"Silly rabbits!" said the owl, and he flew away.

The little rabbit was just calling after him, but when the little rabbit opened his mouth to speak, the bumblebee had curled up to sleep in his throat —— AND —— all he could do was whisper.

"What shall I do?" he whispered to a squirrel who wasn't sleepy.

"Wake him up," said the squirrel. "Wake up the bumblebee."

"How?" whispered the rabbit. "All I can do is whisper and I'm sleepy and I want to go to sleep and who can sleep with a bumblebee —"

Suddenly a wise old groundhog popped up out of the ground.

"All I can do is whisper," said the little rabbit.

"All the better," said the groundhog.

"Come here, little rabbit," he said, "and I will whisper to you how to wake up a bumblebee."

"You have to make the littlest noise that you can possibly make because a bumblebee doesn't bother about big noises. He is a very little bee and he is only interested in little noises."

"Like a loud whisper?" asked the rabbit.

"Too loud," said the groundhog and popped back into his hole.

"A little noise," whispered the rabbit, and he started making little rabbit noises — he made a noise as quiet as the sound of a bird's wing

cutting the air, but the bee didn't wake up. So the little rabbit made the sound of snow falling, but the bee didn't wake up.

So the little rabbit made the sound of a bug breathing and a fly sneezing and grass rustling and a fireman thinking. Still the bee didn't wake up. So the rabbit sat and thought of all the little sounds he could think of— What could they be?

A sound quiet as snow melting, quiet as a flower growing, quiet as an egg, quiet as — And suddenly he knew the little noise that he would make — and he made it.

It was like a little click made hundreds of miles away by a bumblebee in an apple tree in full bloom on a mountain top. It was the very small click of a bee swallowing some honey from an apple blossom.

And at that the bee woke up.

He thought he was missing something, and away he flew.

And then what did the little rabbit do? That sleepy sleepy little rabbit?

He closed his mouth
He closed his eyes
He closed his ears
And he tucked in his paws
And twitched his nose
And he went sound asleep!

RABBIT

POEM

Nobody knows a rabbit's nose
The way it twitches
The way it goes
Constantly on his face

Nobody knows a rabbit's ears
The way he listens
And what he hears
And his sad little rabbit
tears

Nobody knows a rabbit's eyes
Red as rubies without surprise
In his square fur face

ALL THE PRETTY LITTLE HORSES

Go to sleep
Go to sleep
Go to sleepy little baby
When you wake
You shall have
All the pretty little horses

Black and bay
Dapple and gray
All the pretty little horses

Mother loves you

Daddy loves you

Everybody loves baby

The butterflies and the flies

Are buzzing round your eyes

So go to sleepy little baby

And after your sleep

I'll give you a

Jeep

and
All the pretty little horses
Black and bay
Dapple and gray
All the pretty little horses
BABY'S
Go to sleep, Go to sleep, Go to sleep - y, lit - tle ba - by.
When you wake, you shall have All the pret - ty lit - tle hors - es,

Mother loves you
Daddy loves you
Everybody loves baby
SONG
Black and bay, Dapple and gray, All the pret - ty little
hors - es. Mother loves you, Daddy loves you, Ev - ery - bod - y loves Ba - by.

CLOSE YOUR EYES

Little donkey on the hill
Standing there so very still
Making faces at the skies
Little donkey close your eyes.

Silly sheep that slowly crop
Night has come and you must stop
Chewing grass beneath the skies
Silly sheep now close your eyes.

Little monkey in a tree
Swinging there so merrily
Throwing coconuts at the skies
Little monkey close your eyes.

Little birds that sweetly sing
Curve your heads beneath your wing
No more whistling in the skies
Little birds now close your eyes.

Little horses in your stall
Stop your stomping, stop it all
Tails stop switching after flies
Little horses close your eyes.

Little pigs that snuff about
No more snorting with your snout
No more squealing to the skies
Noisy pigs now close your eyes.

Old black cat down in the barn
Keeping four black kittens warm
Winds are quiet in the skies
Dear old black cat close your eyes.

Little child all tucked in bed
Looking like a sleepy head
Stars are quiet in the skies
Little child now close your eyes.

Little donkey, close your eyes.
Silly sheep, now close your eyes.
Little monkey, close your eyes.
Little birds, now close your eyes.
Little horses, close your eyes.
Noisy pigs, now close your eyes.
Dear old black cat, close your eyes.
Little child, now close your eyes.

GOING TO SLEEP

ALL over the world the animals are going to sleep — the birds and the bees, the horse, the butterfly, and the cat.

In their high nests by the ocean the fish hawks are going to sleep. And how does a young fish hawk go to sleep? The same as any other bird in the world.

She folds her wings and pushes herself deep in the nest, looks around and blinks her eyes three times, takes one long last look over the ocean, then tucks her head under her wing and sleeps like a bird.

And the fish in the sea sleep in the darkened sea when the long green light of the sun is gone.

And they sleep like fish, with their eyes wide open in some quiet current of the sea.

And above and beyond under the stars on the land, all the little horses are going to sleep. Some stand up in the still dark fields and some fold their legs under them and lie down. But they all go to sleep like horses.

Even the bees and the butterflies sleep when the moths begin to fly. And they sleep like bees and butterflies, under a leaf or a stick or a stone with folded wings and their eyes wide open. For fish and bees and butterflies and flies never close their shiny eyes.

And the old fat bear in the deep dark woods goes into his warm cave to sleep for the whole winter.

So do the groundhogs and the hedgehogs, the skunks and the black-eyed raccoons. They eat a lot, then sleep until spring, a long warm sleep.